CUTTING THROUGH

Cutting Through

J. Thomas Brown

First Printing, 2025
Beverly Hills Press RVA

1

The Silver Meteor glided silently into Baltimore at 8:15 p.m. Annie hailed a taxi outside the station. "5001 Bayview Boulevard. It's the Hopkins medical annex," she said, sliding into the front seat. The octocopter arrived at the medical center a few minutes later and let her off by the roof entrance. Clear Light Sleep Center was listed in the directory as suite 122. She walked with a lopsided gait to the end of the hall and entered.

The waiting room was decorated in soft shades of blue and dream motifs. Annie signed in and no sooner was seated when Dr. Batsunappen came to greet her. His accent was English with an underlying musical quality.

"I'm Dr. Batsunappen."

She extended a shaky hand. "Annie Taylor."

He was unusually tall. His complexion contrasted with the starched white coat he was wearing. His manner was lively and brisk, not like she imagined a sleep doctor would be. She thought him handsome.

The doctor escorted her down a hallway to his office and motioned to sit. Statues and paintings from Tibet and Indian Vedas and Upanishads adorned the room. One wall held shelves of books on sleeping and neurological disorders.

Dr. Batsunappen sat at his desk and studied Annie with curiosity. He noticed her looking at the sculpture set in the wall behind him. "That is called Vishnu Dreaming the Universe." He swiveled to face the sculpture. "Vishnu is floating on the cosmic ocean, lying on the serpent Ananta. These figures," he said, gesturing to the upper portion, "represent the five senses. The question is, who is dreaming who?"

"Interesting thought," said Annie.

"The nature of dreams and reality has always been a central theme in Indian culture. In the Aka-Upanishad, 3,000 years ago, it was written: 'In dreams, he transcends this world and all forms of death…there are no chariots in that state, no horses, no roads. There are no blessings there, no happiness, no joys, but he himself sends forth blessings, happiness and joys. There are no tanks there, no lakes, no rivers, but he himself sends forth tanks, lakes and rivers. He indeed is the maker.'"

Annie shook her head. "It's very interesting but my problem is I haven't been able to sleep right for months and it's getting worse. I'm exhausted all the time and living in a fog."

Doctor Batsunappen sighed. "Forgive me. We must talk about what is troubling you. When did this start?"

She told him of the pain in her head at work, the periods of double vision and fatigue that followed and her inability to sleep. Her features were wan and sunken and her hands shook. Dark circles hung beneath her eyes. "I've not slept for three days."

He listened intently and nodded from time to time. "Tell me what you mean when you say you haven't slept. Do you first fall asleep then wake up over and over all night? Or are you unable to fall asleep at all?"

"When I begin to fall asleep this sensation of heat pours over me, then I'm filled with pins and needles down my spine and I'm wide awake again. It goes on all night until it hurts." A tear escaped from her right eye and landed on his desk.

He regarded the tear impassively. "You're exhibiting symptoms of severe sleep deprivation and neurological dysfunction. What concerns me is what may be causing it. Some of the symptoms you exhibit are indicative of a problem perhaps in the sleep centers such as the pineal or pons."

He pressed a button on his desk. "Imaging lab."

A nurse appeared on his screen. "Hello, Dr. Batsunappen."

"I have a Ms. Ann Taylor here who needs a head MRI. It's a rush. How's the wait?"

"Twenty minutes."

"I'll send her over shortly." He smiled at Annie. "Before you go, Ms. Taylor, let me show you the lab."

She followed the doctor through the lobby to a door labelled SLEEP LAB and he ushered her inside. The lab was motel-like and filled with equipment at one end where technicians worked at control panels. Two stories of rooms lined the opposite side of the space. "We have one of the largest sleep labs in the country, probably in the world. There're thirty sleeping rooms. Over here we have the monitoring stations; six of them, one for every five patients. They monitor and record the activity in the brain and body during sleep."

"I didn't think it would be such a large operation," said Annie.

He led her into one of the chambers. A night table and chair sat next to a full-sized bed. "The conditions for sleep are better than most people have in their own homes. It appears plain, but in the ceiling are hundreds of receptors and monitoring sensors. Your body functions and brain waves are picked up by the sensors and sent to the nearest station to be recorded and analyzed."

"Aren't there all kinds of wires you have to hook up?"

He opened the table drawer and produced a small box filled with tiny pink buttons. "We place these on your skin to do the monitoring. You won't notice them; there aren't any wires." He smiled reassuringly. "First we have to scan inside your head and see what's going on."

A medical assistant arrived with a wheelchair to take her to Imaging.

After the scan was run Annie was taken back to the reception room and Dr. Batsunappen, a neurologist by training, met in the imaging room with Dr. Mark Payne, a neurosurgeon, to consult.

"Does this look like an abnormality to you?" he asked, pointing to a peanut sized spot as Dr. Payne squinted through the hologram.

Dr. Payne nodded. "Looks like a deep lesion penetrating into the pons."

"What do you think caused it—MS?"

"It looks like the synapses are burned chemically in the affected area. Perhaps a neurotoxin of some kind escaped the blood brain barrier and the myelin and tissue have been damaged. The nerve signals are leaking away to nowhere all the same."

"Yes, but how do we fix it," said Dr. Batsunappen.

Dr. Payne stared into the matrix of light. "You can't cut it out, Raji. I could possibly ablate the scarring with laser surgery but it would be risky."

Dr. Batsunappen turned the matrix off. "The nerve signals would still be disrupted by the absence of myelin with an ablation. The weekly grand round is at nine tomorrow morning. We can discuss her case at the meeting."

Annie was fidgeting in the reception room when Dr. Batsunappen returned. "We just have to get you set up in the lab," he said, helping her to her feet. A technician took her suitcase and led her to a vacant sleeping chamber where she changed into her pajamas. Buttons were placed on her temples, at the corners of her eyes, the sides of her chin, ankles, and numerous other places. The technician left and turned out the light.

Despite the comfortable setting the cycle of sleep disruption repeated and she didn't fall asleep. Shuffling her way through the doorway of the monitoring station, she stood behind the sleep technician who was busy trying to figure out why the recording of wave patterns had stopped.

"I can't sleep. Can you give me something," Annie demanded.

The technician jumped in her seat. "God, you scared me to death."

A warning message popped up on a monitor.

The technician pushed a button. "Mike, its Mr. Harrison in room thirty again." She swiveled her chair to face Annie. "He has terrible dreams. They even give me nightmares."

"I didn't know they were contagious," Annie replied, sarcastically.

She returned her ire. "Of course not, but I've seen them. Dr. Batsunappen hooks up electrodes to his brain that let you see the dreams and we record them."

"Really? Can I see one?"

The technician shook her head. "They're personal. I can't do that."

"You aren't going to record my dreams, are you?"

She scowled. "Not if you're awake."

"Then couldn't I have a sleeping pill or a shot of something?"

"The first night we can't give you anything. We have to log your natural patterns before we try to alter anything. Go back to your room now. Relax. Sleep comes of its own when we aren't trying."

As she rose to guide Annie back, cries came from Mr. Harrison's open door. "Mike, close the door for God's sake." A latch clicked into place and the quiet returned.

Annie tossed for hours. Every time sleep started to come the heat and pins and needles sensation shot through her and brought her back to wakefulness. The pain in her head throbbed relentlessly.

In the morning the technician began pulling off the buttons. "The graphs didn't show any sleep at all."

"Brilliant."

"That's no way to start the day," she said cheerfully. "Have a shower and get something to eat, then you'll feel better."

Annie dropped leadenly into the chair as Dr. Batsunappan slid a box of Kleenex toward her. "What did the tests show, Doctor? Am I fixable?"

He smiled uneasily. "I'll go over what we've found and what the options are for you. Let me be straightforward. The scan showed a lesion in the area of the brain that regulates circadian rhythms. We call your condition an intrinsic dyssomnia."

"You're over my head already."

"There's damage to an area of your brain that regulates sleep. The damaged area tried to heal itself and formed a lesion in the tissue. That's why you're unable to remain asleep. Scar tissue can't conduct nerve impulses. The electrical impulses to the sleep center are leaking away or distorted."

Her shoulders heaved and she wiped at the tears falling from her right eye and down her cheek. "I'm crying from just one eye. I'm so screwed up."

He reached over the desk and patted her hand. "We discussed your condition at a meeting of the university neurologists this morning. Normally this kind of condition can't be corrected. That is—not until now. One of the team members talked about something new that has worked in preliminary tests. It's called RMC. Recombinant metal crystallography. It's a kind of liquid metal that can be directed to the damaged area through the cerebral veins, where we weren't able to get to before, and then be activated to bypass the scar tissue and restore the nerve impulses." Annie pulled her hand away. "I can't believe this is happening to me and what you're telling me. I'll be an experiment."

Dr. Batsunappen looked her in the eye. "It would be much less intrusive than conventional brain surgery. A much faster recovery is expected. The operation would only take an hour, and in a day or so, you could be right as rain. But this is a big decision and you need time to think about it."

"That's not necessary. There doesn't seem to be any other choice."

"Good, I'll make the arrangements," he said reassuringly. "We'll get you transferred from the sleep clinic to the hospital medical center and get you prepped over there. The brain has no feeling or ability to sense pain in itself, so you'll receive a local anesthetic and a sedative prior to the surgery, then brought to the OR. There's no need to be put under for this procedure."

He pressed the com button. "Admissions, please." An office administrator appeared on the screen. "This is Dr. Batsunappen. I need to admit a new patient, Ms. Ann Taylor. Send an aide over, please."

An orderly helped Annie into her wheelchair. It was a long way to her room in the neurological wing. A nurse followed them in and helped Annie change into a hospital gown and climb into bed.

"The operation's at 1:00," said the nurse.

"Can I make some calls?" asked Annie.

"You sure can." The nurse pressed on the side of the bedside table and a com panel popped up. Annie keyed in her mother's number.

"We're coming to see you," said her mother after hearing the troubling news.

"You don't have to. They're taking good care of me. The operation is this afternoon and they say I'll be out of here by tomorrow."

"You're going to need at least a day or two to get back on your feet. Your father and I want to help out, so it's not an option. We'll take the next flight to Baltimore and be there tomorrow afternoon."

The nurse returned pushing a cart containing syringes. "The anesthesiologist will be here in a second to get you ready."

"We love you. Think positive thoughts," her mother said.

"I love you, too." She disconnected.

The anesthesiologist was a wiry man with sunken cheeks and an intense expression. "The liquid metal device will be introduced through an incision in your cranium. I'm going to give you a few shots and get you numb. Do you have any questions you'd like to ask me?"

Annie stared at the syringes. "Will I still be conscious?"

He nodded his head. "Yes, but we're going to make sure you won't feel anything. The local anesthetic in your scalp is followed by a series of sedatives that will allow you to be conscious enough to respond to any questions." He gave Annie an injection in the arm. A pleasant warmth began to spread throughout her body.

The nurse began shaving her hair and Annie laughed as tufts of it fell about her. "You're cutting off my hair, aren't you?"

"We have to honey," she replied, smiling.

After her head was denuded, the anesthesiologist picked up another syringe and made several injections in a circle.

"Feel this?" he asked.

She looked upward as he scratched her scalp. "Nope."

A ubiquitous light with no apparent source filled the Spartan operating room. A nurse and an aide wheeled in Annie and lifted her onto the operating table that sprouted from the middle of the floor. The anesthesiologist inserted a small shunt into the back of her hand, then pulled a tube from the side of the table and attached it to the shunt. Annie watched with curiosity as a clear liquid filled the tube and entered her body.

Two suited physicians entered the OR tugging at their surgical gloves. Despite the surgical dress, hair cap and mask, she recognized the tall frame of Dr. Batsunappen. "I guess this is it, Doctor."

"You're doing just fine." He pointed to his colleague. "This is Dr. Payne, who will be performing your surgery."

She tried to speak but the combination of her exhaustion and the sedative made the choosing of words difficult. It was hard to focus through the haze. "Tell him to go," she said, slurring her words.

Dr. Payne peered down at Annie and laughed. "Could I have some of what she's having? That's how I want to feel."

She tried to sit up but her body wouldn't respond. The paralyzing effect of the drugs had taken hold.

Dr. Batsunappen took her hand. "Sometimes there's a brief panic reaction to the sedative. It will only last a moment. Believe me, you're in the best of hands. Dr. Payne is an outstanding neurosurgeon."

"Soon you'll be sleeping like a baby again," added Dr. Payne. He nodded to the anesthesiologist.

Annie felt the warmth returning, but this time it was stronger. She became detached and didn't care about anything. He wheeled over a laser scalpel that the surgical staff had nicknamed "Gort" and activated a series of metallic curved rods that emerged from the surface of the operating table in a ring about her head. When she was completely locked into position holograms sprang to life, revealing the contents inside her head in detail, along with vectors of vital statistics. Dr. Batsunappen marked her scalp to indicate the point of entry and Dr. Payne trained Gort on the speck of dye. An almond shaped lid opened on the front and a green beam, so thin it was barely visible, emerged from the eye. It grew in length and met with the scalp, then burned deeper into the skull. There was a momentary sizzle before it extinguished. The lid closed silently.

The surgeon pushed the laser away impatiently and picked up a syringe containing the recombinant liquid metal. He inserted the needle into the hole made by the beam.

"You're over the fissure, just a little deeper," said Dr. Batsunappen, watching the hologram intently. "Right there."

Dr. Payne clamped the syringe in place and activated the plunger. "I'm beginning the injection." The liquid resembled mercury as it flowed through the needle into the brain. As it traveled through the complex network of veins it blipped its location, guided magnetically by both doctors until it arrived at a point beside the pons. The integration with living native brain tissue was the most dangerous part of the operation but would only take seconds.

Dr. Batsunappen stood beside her at the operating table and observed her demeanor. "Ms. Taylor, can you hear me?"

She responded from a place far away. "Yes."

He held up three fingers. "How many do you see?" She counted them aloud. "Good. We're activating the program now. You may feel yourself falling asleep suddenly but that's nothing to worry about. Don't fight it." He nodded to Dr. Payne, who removed the syringe from the hole in her skull.

Dr. Batsunappen keyed in a series of program commands at a control panel on the wall. A few seconds later PROGRAM COMPLETE displayed. Annie's eyes widened in surprise and rolled slowly before closing as smoothly as Gort's lid. He studied the displays until the wave patterns transitioned to sleep spindles and K-complexes. "She's entering phase two and going deeper," he announced. "She's sleeping."

The medical crew congratulated one another with smiles and backslaps, ringing Annie as she slept on her lotus petal bed, dreaming dreams of the universe.

The next morning Dr. Batsunappan observed the output from Annie's brain and worried she had not left REM sleep. Her sensors picked up continuous rapid eye movement, sometimes exaggerated and frantic, showing her to be submerged in the deepest level of the dreaming states.

He at first thought it was natural to sleep so long because she had a four-day deficit to make up. She had been in phase four dreaming since the liquid metal device had been activated. Typically, that state would last about fifty-five minutes, then the sleeper would recycle back through the previous stages before re-entering stage four REM again. After three or four iterations of cycling the sleeper should have awakened fully.

An aide entered the monitoring station and informed Dr. Batsunappan that Annie's parents were in the waiting room. "I'll be right there," he said.

He spotted a nervous middle-aged couple sitting near the entrance. Smiling confidently, he introduced himself. "I'm Dr. Batsuappan. Let me take you to her room and I'll explain on the way. It's a bit of a walk, I'm afraid."

"Is this part of the hospital?" her mother asked.

"The sleep center is an adjunct of Hopkins. Your daughter is here because the portion of her brain that controls sleep was damaged and we are the best equipped to deal with her problem."

"How is she? We were told the operation went well," her father said.

"It did." Dr. Batsunappan summed up events after the operation. "She's still sleeping," he explained as they neared her room.

They stopped outside the door. "She said she would be coming home today," said her mother. "Is everything all right?"

This was the part he hated. There were irregularities that he couldn't possibly explain, even if he did have the answers. He put on his best poker face and opened the door, gesturing them to enter. "We expect a full recovery." He had almost dared to hope to find her awake, but the sleep was still profound. It seemed there was no one inhabiting her body. The mystery of consciousness loomed unsolved before him. "I'll leave you with her."

After her parents sat by her bedside watching for half an hour, her father picked up her hand. "Annie, we're here." There was no response.

An hour went by and a nurse came in with a cart. "I need to check a few things. We only let people stay for an hour after surgery," she said, tugging on the privacy curtains.

Her mother kissed her on the forehead. "We love you, Annie," she said as they rose to go.

Dr. Payne joined Dr. Batsunappan in the monitoring room the second morning after the operation. "How is she?"

The sleep doctor nervously tapped on the display. "There's another piece to the puzzle we don't understand yet. She's exhibiting continuous rapid eye movement, sometimes frantic. That indicates nightmares."

"What are you saying?"

Dr. Batsunappen regarded his colleague sadly. "Usually a change occurs in chemical and electrical activity in the central nervous system that releases the sleeper from sleep paralysis but hers is missing. She's unable to awaken."

Dr. Payne bit his lip. "If we can't reprogram the implant, we'll have to develop some sort of reverse procedure to undo everything. God knows how long that will take."

"Come with me," said Dr. Batsunappen. His colleague had difficulty keeping up. They walked to the far end of the hall to the last room. A man lay on his back, pallid and sunken. A bundle of wires ran from the top of his shaven head to a small black box. The box was the size of a box of tissues; black and smooth with an on-off switch and a plug that contained the cable that was wired into the patient's skull. On the wall hung a large display panel. The patient appeared to be asleep, although his breathing was weak and irregular.

"This is John Harrison," said Dr. Batsunappen. "He was diagnosed with advanced cancer when he was brought in. He has no insurance or financial assistance and volunteered to help us in our research."

"What research?"

Dr. Batsunappan studied his colleague cautiously. "Dream research. Cancer produces psychological trauma. Fear of dying often results in disturbed sleep with nightmares. With the research conducted here I've been able to develop a tool to heal sleep disorders. A dream portal."

"A what?" His eyes darted back and forth over the neurologist's face.

"Conventional neurology teaches our brains are compartmentalized and mapped. That each part has a specific function and the billions of memory cells contain specific memories hard coded to certain locations. We're taught we only use 10% and it's impossible to understand its complexity."

"I get it. That's what we all learned in school."

Dr. Batsunappan patted his colleague's arm reassuringly. "Myths. The brain is not hard coded at all. It's an open-ended receiver and transmitter that's based on electrical signals. It's bi-directional and I'm able to read the electrical signals generated during sleep and redirect the output to a display screen. The signals convert to real time imagery so that we can see a live dream as it happens. They can be recorded and played back to regenerate the dream."

Dr. Payne shook his head in disbelief.

"I know it's asking a lot for you to accept the idea but it's true." Dr. Batsunappen plugged an output from the box to the display screen. "Watch."

Images began to form, then voices were discernible. The outlines sharpened until the dream began to congeal. The images were at first eidetic and cartoonish, then became smoother in motion and more realistic in color. It played like a movie on the screen:

John Harrison stood in a small garden shed with a dozen people who were younger than himself. They milled about aimlessly in the overcrowded shed until the door splintered outward and burst. Harrison and the others fell out into a lake and swam to a motorboat, climbing over the sides until the boat began to sink. The patient thrashed in the water as the dream continued playing on the screen.

"It doesn't make much sense to us but it's important to him," said Dr. Batsunappen.

"It's like a portal to another world," said Dr. Payne in astonishment.

"I'll hook up Ann Taylor and use it to control her nightmares. Will you help me?"

"We should discuss this at the round table first."

Dr. Batsunappen frowned, shaking his head. "She's going through hell. We have to act now."

They worked quickly to disconnect Mr. Harrison from the dream portal and placed the equipment on a cart. After wheeling it to Annie's room, Dr. Payne ordered a local anesthetic. He administered several injections around the incision made by Gort. Carefully cutting away the freshly healed skin over the opening, he inserted the wire lead from the dream portal into the hole in the bone that was now exposed.

Dr. Batsunappen turned on the dream portal. "Isn't it ironic that we are looking today into the land of dreams, the place of magic and prophecy for thousands of years—with science?" Her eyes darted frantically beneath her lids and the screen brightened. Images formed, then sharpened and deepened in color.

They watched intently through the lens of Annie's mind's eye. The camera swooped down on massive iron gates at the front entrance of a great estate. A private road bordered by brooding pines ran through an expanse of lawn to a large gray stone house at the far end. The dreamscape was locked in the grip of winter. The camera took them inside the house where Annie and her parents congregated in the living room.

She looked through a window onto the lawn as billowing clouds poured over the horizon. They blanketed the estate and house, casting the interior into darkness.

"We have to go right now," shouted Annie. All three occupants ran outside, Annie in the lead. She led them down the driveway to the gates. Before they reached them, the gates swung open and admitted a black hearse that streaked toward the house. It generated a whooshing noise as it cut through the air. The hearse stopped suddenly at a garden walkway and the back hatch swung open to emptiness.

"Faster," screamed Annie. As she ran down the path it became evident her legs were becoming weaker with each stride. She slowed to a lopsided lope, struggling to continue. Rounding a curve in the path, she came to a pit, a moss lined hole in the earth the size of a swimming pool. Something was moving down in the pit.

The physicians watched her fear vectors display on a monitor in terms of heartbeat and respiration and hormonal levels. "Look at the output, she's under great stress. It's real to her. We've got to get her out of this," said Dr. Batsunappen, angrily.

Her fear drew her like a magnet to the edge of the pit. She spoke to whatever was lurking in the hole. "Show yourself. I know you're there. I'm not afraid of you."

A form began to rise over the side. As it climbed the stress graphs redlined, belying her words. The face was that of a gaunt and emaciated creature whose sallow skin was nearly rotten. The dark hollows of its eyes spoke disease. The figure stood, towering over Annie. It lifted a long-sleeved arm, the cloth of its coat falling back to expose a fleshless hand. The face leered as the hand extended. Annie put out her own in self-defense. The thing was stronger than she was. When her hand met its fleshless bones it began to push her into the earth with a supernatural force. The mossy ground parted about her useless legs and swallowed them up a few inches at a time.

"Someone help—help me, please," she pleaded.

"Do no harm," said Dr. Batsunappen, unable to break away from the scene.

"We should not interfere, Raji. She needs to resolve it in her own way."

"If you're thinking it doesn't matter because it's only a dream, you're full of crap."

Dr. Payne looked down at Annie on the bed. Her lips moved, allowing inarticulate moans to escape. "She's your patient. What do you want to do?"

"I can help her take control of her dreams to ease her through this until we come up with the implant solution. I'll teach her to use a Tibetan technique I know."

"She's asleep! How the hell will you teach her anything?" He sneered contemptuously, convinced of his colleague's insanity.

Dr. Batsunappan picked up the lead to the display panel and thrust it at Dr. Payne. "Hook it up to the audio-video."

The neurosurgeon stepped sideways and reached for the red emergency button instead.

"Don't. Trust me. Hook it up, please, Mark."

Dr. Payne clenched his teeth and plugged in the cable. Dr. Batsunappen plugged the other end into the input of the dream portal, then keyed in commands. He stepped back to place his body in view of the built-in lens of the display and appeared standing next to Annie in full view of the phantasm. He moved to one side so that she could see him better and the phantasm lifted its bony hand from hers and stared silently at him. The physician glowed like an angel of mercy against the cold barrenness of the dreamscape.

"Help me doctor. Get me out of here, please," she sobbed.

The physician forced himself to bury his emotions. "Ms. Taylor, the operation wasn't a success. The release mechanism isn't working and you can't wake up. I need to show you a way to deal with this until we can make the adjustments to the implant."

"No, no. Get me out. Can't you help me?"

The creature advanced to Annie and resumed forcing her back into the soil.

"Ignore that thing," said Dr. Batsunappen. "It's made from you."

She couldn't tear away from its boney glare. "It won't let me go."

"I know it seems hard but if you use your will, it's possible. You can take control of this dream and all the others. You'll have to do exactly as I tell you. Once you know how, you can make your own dreams. You can be The Maker. Remember the verse I told you? 'In dreams, he transcends this world and all forms of death…he himself sends forth blessings, happiness and joys. He is The Maker.'"

"I remember you explaining the sculpture. Who is dreaming who, you said."

"Repeat these words with all your will power, with all your intent. Don't hesitate in your conviction: I will awaken within the dream and know that I am dreaming."

Annie looked into Dr. Batsunappen's wild eyes, repeating the words.

"Say it again."

She continued repeating it a second and third time.

"Good. Hold out your hands in front of you. Look down at them and watch them closely." Annie held out her hands and looked down. "Do you understand that they are your hands in your dream?"

"I do."

"Now turn them over slowly so your palms are face up."

Annie obeyed. The creature stepped back and watched through sunken eyeholes.

"Do you understand that you have moved your hands in your dream with your own will?" She nodded. "Yes, I moved them with my will." "Now, look down at your legs. Do you understand that they are your legs in your dream?" She nodded again. "I understand." "Then use your will to lift them out of the soil. They're your legs and subject to your will." Annie pulled her right leg upward. The soil formed a suction that resisted her efforts, but the leg slowly lifted, an inch at a time, until her entire leg was free. She pulled upward on her other leg, repeating the process until she stood with both feet on top the mucky soil. Her lips trembled and tears ran down her cheeks.

"The rest is up to you. Make your own way through your world now. You are The Maker." He nodded to his colleague.

"Bravo, Raji," said Dr. Payne, disconnecting the plug.

Annie stared at the empty space where Dr. Batsunappen had stood. She turned to face the phantasm. It leered at her, waiting. She forced her legs into motion and began running, slipping and falling at first, then gaining speed, leaving the pit behind.

She climbed a stone wall and ran into thick woods. The presence of the thing was behind her as she pushed through saplings and thorns to escape it. When she came to Silver Lake, where she had skated as a girl, the primordial presence stopped at the shoreline. She glided onto the ice and willed skates on her feet. With a sideways shove she pushed her weight into motion. It became night and the moon reflected across the frozen surface in a shimmering streak of blue moonbeams. Under the moon her graceful form danced in harmony with the night, her happiness deepening as she leapt into the air spinning and free.

2

The door swung partly open and a nurse leaned halfway into the room. "Ann Taylor's parents are here. Should I tell them to come back later?"

Dr. Batsunappan rubbed his forehead to erase the image of the phantasm from his mind. He glanced at his watch. "Show them to my office."

Dr. Payne waited for the door to close. "What did I just see a few minutes ago? Am I to believe you were communicating directly with the mind of another human being or was that some sort of prerecorded hoax?"

"It was no stunt, Mark," said Dr. Batsunappan indignantly. He looked down at Annie lying on the bed. "We're at the cusp of something larger than ourselves. Consciousness never sleeps, it's always at work. During the day it guides us through the world to ensure our physical survival. In our sleep it's assembling the events and experiences of our waking world into the personality that we call the self. The inner world becomes the outer world. My portal is a machine that can pierce through the organic barrier of the brain into the electricity of the self-aware mind. Consciousness is electrical. There's no doubt that we'll be able to communicate at all stages of consciousness, including the wakeful states."

Dr. Payne dragged a chair to Annie's bedside and sat down beside her. "I never thought of it that way. It's just that it hasn't sunk in completely. But I've gone from total cynic to … maybe. This might be the greatest breakthrough in medical technology in a hundred years."

"My paper is coming out in the *Journal of Neurology* next month. I need all the backing I can get."

Dr. Payne smiled ruefully. "But for now, we have to find out what went wrong with the implant."

"I need a team on this. I'll bring in the whole department if I have to."

"That means Gottlieb, too."

Dr. Batsunappan patted his colleague on the back and turned to go. "Even old Gottlieb. Thanks for your help. I do need your support. Excuse me, the Taylors are waiting."

The Taylors' patience had stretched thin. He felt the tension in the air as he sat down at his desk. "I apologize for making you wait. I know how stressful this is for you."

"Why can't we see her?" her father demanded.

"Your daughter hasn't awakened yet. We're conducting tests this morning to determine what's causing her condition."

"Condition?" said her mother. "What condition?"

Dr. Batsunappan shifted back in his seat. "Mrs. Taylor, let me start over. Although it may be unusual to sleep so long after brain surgery, this isn't the first time it's happened. Actually, the term can refer to a state of well-being, too. Her vital signs are good, but she has not yet awakened."

"It's after eleven now. Can we see her?" her father asked.

The doctor cringed at the thought of their reaction to seeing wires sprouting from her head into the dream portal. "We're still running the tests. Come back this evening."

They grunted their consent and rose to leave. "Wait a minute," said Dr. Batsunappan. "It's good that you're here. We need to look into possible causes of the lesion. I don't see her occupation mentioned in her history. What does she do for a living?"

"She's a stockbroker," said Mrs. Taylor.

He keyed the information into his computer. "Any hobbies? Pastimes?"

"She loved to ice skate but when she was training for the national championship she broke her ankle. It never healed the same." Mrs. Taylor glanced at her husband.

"She's a motorhead. Likes to work on her sports car."

"Anything else I should know?"

He looked at his wife and shook his head sadly.

"I'm sorry to hear about the ankle," said Dr. Batsunappan. "Skating for the championships takes a lot of talent." He chuckled as he updated the patient record. "Sports car. That's cool."

After they left, he contacted Brenton Technologies, the company that had written the software for the liquid metal device. They agreed to send a senior programmer in the morning to examine the procedure and to find a way to reprogram the device if necessary. Dr. Batsunappan informed several of his colleagues in the neurology department of what had happened and asked them to come and observe his patient firsthand. They were to assemble at nine the following morning in the monitoring station.

He worked on updating Annie's progress notes and the records of his other patients. Later that afternoon, he and Annie's nurse put the dream portal in a closet, then swaddled her head so that the wires were hidden. He instructed the nurse to let the Taylors visit until eight o'clock, then left for the day.

Dr. Batsunappan arrived at the sleep center half an hour early the next morning to reconnect her to the dream portal, then went to the monitoring station. While waiting for the team to assemble, he checked Annie's readouts. During his twenty years as a neurologist, he had on rare occasions witnessed the impossible, and he had not given up hoping for just one more miracle. One patient of his had meningitis caused by e coli bacteria. The bacteria had destroyed the neocortex and the man was declared brain dead. The prognosis was five years or less on life support as a vegetable. On the fifth day of vegetative state the family met at the patient's bedside to discuss disconnecting him when his eyes suddenly opened and he called out, I'm still here. A month later he had fully recovered.

Dr. Batsunappan was frowning over her EEG when the others arrived; Dr. George Gottlieb, head of neurology, Dr. Carol Lyons, a neuropsychiatrist, Dr. Payne, and Dr. Laticia Green, the senior programmer from Brenton.

"Well, doctor, what do you have for us?" asked Dr. Gottlieb, peering at the readout from behind Dr. Batsunappan.

Startled, Dr. Batsunappan turned to face them. "Dr. Latricia Green, from Brenton. I'm not a medical doctor," she said, sticking out her hand. "PhD in biomedical programming. Call me Latrice."

Dr. Batsunappan pumped her arm vigorously. "Thank you for coming on such short notice, Latrice. Hello Dr. Lyons."

"I got your memo, but I still don't have a clear idea yet what's going on."

Dr. Batsunappan went over the medical history in detail, hoping Latrice could keep up, then turned to Dr. Gottlieb. "You'll notice on the readout there has been no change for over two days."

The older physician shook his head. "Never saw anything like it before. The wave patterns indicate continuous REM 4. Paradoxical sleep."

"This is certainly not a coma," said Dr. Lyons. "Accelerated heartbeat and respiration. Constant synchronized eye movement. She's dreaming her ass off."

Dr. Batsunappan smiled wryly. "Would you like to see what's going on inside her head right now?" He watched the expression on everyone's face with amusement.

"He's not joking," said Dr. Payne.

They followed him to Annie's room where she lay on the bed breathing heavily, sometimes mumbling unintelligibly. "This is Ann Taylor," he said.

Dr. Gottlieb bent down level with the dream portal and eyed it closely. "Is this it? The neuro-communicator?"

"I call it a neuro-translator, but that's it," said Dr. Batsunappan. "Show us."

They stood at the foot of the bed and watched the screen over the headboard as he switched it on.

In the twilight of the dead of winter Annie skated on Silver Lake. Gaining speed, she spun backward and pirouetted into the air. As she was spinning, her body flickered into nothingness. The frigid scene dissolved and she was hovering in the air against a warm summer backdrop over an empty stretch of country highway. An antique sports car purred down the road with the top down and two people inside. The conscious being with no body that was Annie followed behind the car, then connected. She became the passenger, but her dream sheath was her high school self. The driver was Dennis Ropeson, her high school boyfriend. It was still getting dark and they were in a mystery sports car rally in his antique MGA convertible that smelled oily and rattled on the hard pavement. They were on the back roads surrounded by expanses of rolling farmland.

She was the navigator, reading from a list of clues in the form of riddles that determined the route of the race. "It says, turn west of the water tower, then prepare to get a shower."

"Do you see a water tower?" Dennis asked.

"Not really."

"We're lost. Let's pull over and look at the map."

She shrugged. "Okay."

Dennis pulled to the shoulder but instead of taking a map out of the trunk he produced a blanket and spread it on the grass. Smiling, he plunked down.

"Dennis, you don't have a map," she said.

"I don't know where it went. I must have forgotten it."

She sat down beside him anyway. He put his arms around her and gave her a slow kiss, which she returned. Suddenly a brilliant streak of light flashed over the horizon.

"Wow, what was that?" asked Annie. "A meteor."

Two more shot through the twilight trailing long ribbons of bright light that illuminated the sky.

"Wow!" they exclaimed in unison as hundreds more rained down upon the field near them. The dazzling streaks of luminosity were numen of enlightenment, promising answers to all the questions the human race had sought since the beginning of the great whatever.

Dennis leapt up and ran across the road to the field where the meteors appeared to hit. She ran after him, close at his heels.

"Wow, wow!"

The meteors transmuted into flying globes humming with energy. One of the craft hovered over Dennis and pulsed vibrantly, encircling him in buzzing rings of light. He ascended slowly up to the globe inside the rings, writhing in ecstasy while calling to Annie. "Annie, Annie, they know it all. Come join them, it's wonderful."

Another found her and encircled her too. As she ascended, she felt peace and harmony. The warm light promised the answers she longed for. She could join and be one with them. It was a matter of just letting go. The globe emanated wordless reassurances of kindness and eternal contentment, coaxing her. She wanted to so much. But then came a nagging doubt. It held her back from giving in.

"Don't. Dennis, don't. You won't be you anymore. You'll lose your free will."

Dennis disappeared through the iris in the belly of the craft and was gone. As soon as Annie understood what the globe wanted it rejected her. The rings retracted and she fell. She hit the earth rolling and ran to escape the other globes swooping down on her like angry birds.

A hot burst of light hit a rock nearby and it exploded, showering her with fragments. She zigzagged across the field. Then she remembered she was The Maker and stopped cold. Annie looked at her hands, turning the palms upward. *These are my hands in my dream, and subject to my will.* She closed her eyes and breathed deeply. Gathering all her will power, she said aloud: "Pull out."

The screen blanked. "What the hell?" said Gottlieb. As they gaped, white noise filled in the display, then coalesced into the image of Annie spinning back down to the surface of Silver Lake. Unaware of her audience, she smiled happily and did a triple Lutze in the moonlight.

Dr. Batsunappan switched off the portal and faced the team, expecting cheers or an ovation. They remained staring at the blank screen in silent astonishment. "Any questions or comments?" he asked.

"The lake must be a sort of psychological mechanism for her. A place where she feels safe," said Dr. Lyons. "That was very personal and private. I felt like a voyeur."

"It's a milestone," said Dr. Payne. "It has applications far beyond medical use."

Dr. Gottlieb snorted condescendingly. "Very impressive show, but it's not going to save this patient. I want you all to meet me in the conference room. Dr. Batsunappan, do what you need to do to get her disconnected, then join us."

3

D r. Gottlieb held up his hand for silence. "Does anyone else have reservations about what they just witnessed in there, or am I the only one? Dr. Lyons, I think I detected a note of concern on your part. You said you felt like a voyeur."

She eyed him pensively. "This neuro-translator might revolutionize psychiatry. It's amazing. A blessing, if we can believe everything we just saw. But on the other hand, it's like spying on someone's mind. We have to be careful."

"Raji is going to release his paper to the *Journal of Neurology* in a few weeks," said Dr. Payne. "More testing needs to be done, and when scientifically verified, we can proceed to the ethical considerations. There will have to be new rules, I'm sure."

Gottlieb hunched forward. "Who here has looked at Ms. Taylor's medical chart?"

"I did," said Dr. Payne. "Before and after the round table to operate on her lesion. It's SOP."

"Was there a consent signature for the neuro-communicator procedure?"

Dr. Payne stared blankly and chewed the inside of his cheek. "For the neuro-*translator*? No. I didn't see one."

Gottlieb paused dramatically. "There is no patient consent form to perform the operation."

"I clearly remember her signature approving the experimental use of recombinant liquid metal for her lesion. Can't it be considered as an extension?"

Dr. Batsunappan appeared in the doorway and the smile on his face faded. He had hoped for a more enthusiastic greeting.

The white-haired physician pointed to an empty seat. "Can you explain why there isn't a consent signature for Ann Taylor's neuro-communicator procedure? Which by the way, hasn't been approved for testing yet."

He straightened in his seat and smiled incredulously at Gottlieb. "Of course. She was unconscious."

"There was an entry into the family history made the next day after you interviewed her parents. Why didn't you obtain *their* consent as next of kin?"

Dr. Batsunappan looked around the table imploringly and came to rest on Dr. Lyon. He hoped for her backing more than anyone else's.

She shook her head disapprovingly. "It's a privacy violation without consent, Raji."

"Dr. Batsunappan," said Gottlieb, "I'm taking this matter to the medical ethics board immediately. I suggest you don't practice medicine until we have a decision from them. Are there more violations of other patients we need to worry about?"

"You can't do this. Because of the paperwork? What about my patients?"

Gottlieb shook his finger in Raji's face. "You think not? What about your patients? They need protection from half-baked idiots like you. That's why there are rules."

"What about Annie Taylor?"

"You and Dr. Payne will share your records and notes with Latrice so she may reprogram the implant. Is that okay with you, Latrice?"

Latrice coughed, then forced a strained smile. "If that's what's needed, of course, Doctor. But this isn't going to be simple. I'll need the transcripts of the operation and the subsequent patient data. Now that I know the extent of the problem, I'll need to share the data with two of my programmers…"

Gottlieb frowned at Dr. Batsunappan and turned to Dr. Payne. "You see that the HIPAA requirements are taken care of so they can have access to the patient records."

Dr. Payne nodded.

The senior physician pushed himself away from the table and rose. "Okay. Let's get going."

Dr. Batsunappan returned to the sleep disorders center lost in thought and didn't hear the receptionist's greeting when he walked by her. He slumped down in his office chair and swiveled around to face the sculpture of Vishnu Dreaming the Universe. The dream portal was the culmination of years of work. If the journal accepted the science behind it, he would receive wide recognition and acclaim. There could be grants and funding to follow. Clear Light Technologies had the potential to explode onto the stock market. Or it could topple without the right vision to guide it. The meeting played like a bad movie inside his head. He hadn't seen it coming but it was too surreal not to be real.

He swiveled back and called the receptionist. "I'm not taking patients this afternoon. I have an emergency to deal with. When Dr. Payne and Latricia Green arrive send them to my office."

They spent the afternoon reviewing the records of the operation and the deviated sleep patterns recorded in the lab. Dr. Batsunappan gave her all the information he had. Latricia believed the insulative properties of myelin were not being properly reproduced and took the data back to Brenton Technologies for further study. After adjusting the code, Brenton would need months of testing on live animals before trying it again on a human.

Dr. Batsunappan slumped back in his chair. "That's too long. Can't you fast track it?"

"That's with fast tracking. The time requirements are closely regulated," she replied. "It's late and I got to get going. We'll start on it first thing tomorrow morning."

Dr. Payne remained behind. "Raji, I have to tell you something. Gottlieb spoke to the State Board of Physicians and there's going to be an investigation. They sent someone to pick up the dream portal as evidence. I have to appear at the preliminary hearing tomorrow."

"He isn't blaming you, too, is he?"

"No. It's for questioning. Gottlieb's just got it in for you. I don't have any choice in this."

Dr. Batsunappan massaged his temples. "Poor Annie. Who's going to save her?"

"I believe in what you're doing." He put his hand on his colleague's shoulder. "You will."

"Tell them the truth. Don't worry about me. This is a disaster of my own making." He opened his desk drawer and pulled out a memory stick. "This is for the future. If things go bad, I want you to have it."

Dr. Payne turned it over in his hand. "What do you mean, if it goes bad? What is this?"

"Dream Portal 2.0. The next leap. All the new circuitry and programming. I see where Gottlieb is going. He wants to try to bury my work and I don't want that to happen. I'll save my manuscript to it and leave it where you can find it. It needs to get out into the world. Will you help me?"

"Ah, he's just an old throwback. You're going to win this."

"I have a bad feeling about it. The waking world is not a logical place. Promise to keep it safe from the Gottliebs out there."

Dr. Payne handed it back. "I have to get home to my family."

"You're a lucky man," he replied wistfully.

Dr. Batsunappan wasn't hungry but if he waited until later the restaurants would be closed. It was a problem he had as a bachelor. His work consumed all his time, day and night. He ate as a necessity to keep his energy up, sometimes missing meals. The pattern extended into middle age. Life was still rewarding but at times a loneliness would set in. He wondered if he had made some incorrect assumptions about who he was and where he was going. Caring for his patients gave him satisfaction but it was research that made him happiest and that helped fill the void the most.

He rose from his desk and turned out the lights. As he walked by Annie's monitoring station the technician called out, "Doctor, there's something weird about Ann Taylor's graphs. Can you take a look?"

He traced back over the readings for the last hour. The usual sawtooth and theta oscillations were there, followed by brief explosions of nightmare activity. Then long stretches of what seemed to be static filled the screen.

"I ran diagnostics and everything's working fine," said the technician. "The electrodes are, too. Her vital signs are good."

The doctor rubbed his chin. "The static has rhythmic spaces inside it. Like a pulse. Let's add a Z axis to graph time." He motioned to the technician to give up his seat and typed in the new coordinate mapping. An oscillating double helix pattern emerged on the screen. "This is rich. But what does it mean?"

He walked briskly to Annie's room. Her eyes were closed and the breathing even. Her expression was serene. He had the feeling that no one was inhabiting her body; that there was a dissolution of personality. If only he still had the portal.

"I'll be back to check on her in the morning," he told the technician. "Call me if there any more developments." His self-doubts and worries about the investigation were forgotten by the time he walked out of the clinic.

As he feared, there were no restaurants open, so he microwaved a frozen dinner when he got home. While he sat peacefully chewing, he realized Annie's helix patterns signified a new level of consciousness; something beyond theta and deep REM. It had been days since he had communicated with her and he needed to reach her. He remembered Lama Sri Dorbu, the Tibetan dream monk who had told of his journeys into the dream world and had mastered sheath jumping. The monk taught his followers the way to relinquish the covering of the spirit within and travel through the other world guided by the will. When encountering other dream beings it was possible to enter their sheaths and exist as another. There was a danger to this, however, the monk had cautioned. With too many jumps, the way back to the dreamer's own covering would be lost, and the dreamer could not return to the waking world.

Dr. Batsunappan was confident in his own abilities as an oneironaut. He had traveled in the dream world and approached other beings before. Several times he had become filled with an intense curiosity about them and contemplated jumping their sheaths. He had never taken the final leap, however. He lacked the courage and had always pulled out of the dream from fear of losing the way back.

Ann Taylor had incubated his intellectual curiosity to the point where he was willing to try Lama Sri Dorbu's ancient technique. He lay down on his bed on his right side, pulled up his knees slightly, then rested his torso on his arm and his head on his opened palm. Closing his eyes so the lids were compressed together gently, he concentrated on the points of light on the back of them. Inhaling slowly, a faint mandala formed in his field of vision. His inner voice chanted, *may I awaken within this dream and grasp the fact that I am dreaming, so that all dreamlike beings may likewise awaken from the nightmare of illusory suffering and confusion.* He repeated the prayer twice more, strengthening his intention to awaken within the dream each time.

The moon rose between his eyes and he felt the energy within his body rise to meet it. Then he was hovering, moving through the underbrush of a thick wood until he broke through at the shore of Silver Lake. He willed his body to form and held out his hands, palms upward, to the moon. On the surface of the moon a figure appeared. Its reflection played across the frozen expanse of ice and Annie skated toward him atop it, leaving snakes of shaven ice behind her as she approached.

"Welcome, Doctor!" she cried. "It's been so long. Why didn't you come sooner?"

She looked radiant in a tight-fitting skating suit covered with sequins that sparkled like stars. Something was different about her. She was stronger and more confident.

"I wanted to. But things have changed in the other world." He was unsure how to explain the double helix to a patient. "I wanted to check on you. Are you okay?"

Annie laughed. "I've never been better in my life.

Things have changed in this world, too."

"I want you to tell me about it, but first, I must let you know that I can't be your doctor anymore. Dr. Gottlieb has taken charge of you …." There was the sound of branches breaking. Something large and dark pushed through the trees behind him. He forced himself not to look. Dr. Batsunappan realized that he was the source of the disturbance.

Annie saw it, too, and skated to the edge of the ice thrusting her hands out toward him. "You better get on the ice, Doctor."

"I can't skate, Annie."

"You can do whatever you want. You taught me about The Maker. Remember?"

He looked down and willed skates on his feet. As he glided onto the ice the thing resorbed into the woods. "Will you teach me to skate?"

She took his hands and began skating backward, pulling him along. "But you already know how. No fear." She released him like ammunition from a sling and he shot forward. He skated on his own beside her. A happy smile spread across the older man's face which he quickly erased in embarrassment. "I want you to know that programmers are working on the device that was implanted in you. But it may be a long time until they can apply a fix. It's something about the regulations…"

They stopped together in a shower of ice. "Don't try to save me. I'm not going back. There are more worlds in this place than you can conceive of. Dreams of dreams, world after world. Let me show them to you."

The doctor saw the joy in her face and didn't know what to say. He shook his head slowly. "There are things I must do. I have to go back."

"Are you too old to hope? Those *things* are an illusion."

He frowned sternly. "I'm fifteen years your senior and I am telling you that you will return to the real world. I will tell you what an illusion is and what it is not. We are going to save you."

"No, Doctor. Who will save you from yourself? You can return to your world of brick and mortar if you want to, but not me."

She skated toward the moon and disappeared into its light. The dreamscape shimmered and dissipated. Dr. Batsunappan heard his phone ringing and picked it up on the last ring. It was 3 a.m.

"We lost the readout completely, but her vitals are fine," said the technician. "We switched over to another station. Same thing."

"I'm on my way," said the doctor.

It was still dark when he arrived at the clinic. Dr. Batsunappan grunted his greeting and hurried down the hall to Annie's room. Her body was glowing with health as he looked down upon her, but once more it didn't seem inhabited. He returned to the monitoring station and scrutinized the last hour of readouts. The double helix corresponded to the brief period when he had entered her dream on the lake.

"Is she okay?" asked the technician. "What's going on?"

"I don't know. It could be an interaction with the liquid metal implant. I'm not sure. Keep a close eye out for any more changes."

He was the first one in the cafeteria and had to wait for the coffee to finish brewing. After breakfast he went to his office and checked his patients' records to make sure all the i's were dotted and the t's crossed. Putting off Mr. Harrison's for last, he went through the cancer patient's records thoroughly to reassure himself that the consent form had been filled out properly. He realized with a sinking heart that the neuro-translator had not been identified as an experimental medical device and every byte of information on the use of it had left a time-stamped electronic trail back to him.

The medical board was probably pouring over Harrison's records at this moment. And Ann Taylor's as Mark Payne was answering their questions.

Dr. Batsunappan opened his manuscript for the Journal of Neurology and scrolled to where he had left off. It was nearly ready to submit. Mark was on his side and would have the plans for the new dream portal. It gave him a sense of satisfaction that he and his one ally could beat the old white hair to the punch and prove him to be the doddering reactionary that he was.

He began a new chapter: The Fallacy of Brain Mapping. Late in the afternoon the mail chime sounded. A registered letter had arrived from the State of Maryland Medical Board of Examiners. He was to appear before them immediately to formally surrender his license to practice. In the interim he was disbarred from practicing medicine and was to turn over all patients and records to Dr. John Gottlieb.

He clasped his hands together and took several deep breaths. Anger would serve no purpose. Gottlieb needed to be told to step aside for progress and innovation. He was the one to tell him. The old throwback needed to know that he should not harbor grudges against those who had a future because he had no vision himself. Dr. Batsunappan called the senior physician's office to tell him these things but there was no answer. The white hair had already gone home.

Dr. Batsunappan returned to his writing and continued to work late into the night. When the chapter was finished, he saved it to the memory stick and shut off the computer. He clasped the stick and walked to the window. Outside was the world of brick and mortar. The old Queen Ann row houses of Baltimore lined the streets several stories below the high rise medical center, their lights winking in the darkness. He realized his demise would lead to the appointment of a new director for Clear Light Sleep Technologies and that in all probability it would not survive.

He turned off the office lights and walked to the monitoring station for Annie. Her readout had not changed. "Still the same, Doctor," said the technician. "Have you figured it out?"

He smiled wryly. "Perhaps. Check me into Room 11 next to hers. I'm too tired to drive home." Dr. Batsunappan walked wearily to Room 11 and shut the door. He set the storage device containing his finished paper on the night table where it would be noticed by his colleague. He lay on the empty bed. Pulling his knees up, he rested his head on his opened palm, inhaling and exhaling slowly. He was very tired and immediately the mandala formed in his field of vision. *May I awaken within this dream and grasp the fact that I am dreaming, so that all dreamlike beings may likewise awaken from the nightmare of illusory suffering and confusion.*

Before he had a chance to chant a second time the moon rose, and he flew up to greet it. The sleep doctor passed through and appeared on the shore of Silver Lake and held up his palms. "Annie." Looking across the frozen lake, the stillness of winter warmed his heart. He glided in silence over the blue moonbeams painted into the ice, gaining speed, calling her name.

For a moment he gazed at the stars, amazed at their fullness sparkling in infinity. When he looked down, she was beside him.

"Doctor, you've come. I have so much to show you."

"I'm not a doctor anymore. Call me Raji."

4

Annie dug in her toes and jolted them both to a stop. "How can you not be a doctor anymore?"

He regarded her sadly. "I lost my license. They took it away over a technicality. And the neuro-translator portal I used to teach you lucid dreaming. It seems I didn't dot all my I's and cross all the T's in the paperwork. I've failed you, I'm so sorry."

The ice groaned beneath their combined weight and cracks fanned out in all directions. A dark mass began to unfold from the bushes behind them on the shore. She grabbed his hands and pulled him away from the thin ice. "But, if they took the portal, then how did you get in my dream? Or am I in your dream? I'm terribly confused."

"Ordinarily, the dream state is experienced only in the mind of the dreamer with the memories and senses of that unique self, but in your case, I am in your mind. I believe that what we are experiencing reflects a reality beyond ourselves, in a sense, an experience of transcendental reality. The truth is that consciousness is not isolated to the self but is everywhere. We are in a transpersonal reality created by you."

She cocked her head, gaping. "Transpersonal?"

"I'm in your dream, Annie. I entered with a yoga technique using the image of the moon as a threshold. By crossing over, it led me straight to you in your dreamscape. The reason it works isn't clear. It must have something to do with your double helix sleep pattern the synthetic pons is creating. Your pons is a major part of the brainstem. Besides regulating sleep cycles and REMS, it's vital in connecting the cerebrum and cerebellum. Somehow the liquid metal is allowing me to access your memory—your reality."

She lengthened her stride, increasing their speed. Her gaze rose to the moon hanging above them. "I don't have a reality. There are many worlds in this place. Just one reality is—dull. Now I make all the realities I want."

"Reality is something we believe in during a specific moment in time. Dreamers are confined only by the limit of their imaginations and the strength of their intentions." He followed her line of sight over his shoulder and locked on the moon. "Show me how you do it. Teach an old dog some new tricks."

Annie laughed lightheartedly. "It's not about rituals; it's about believing and not letting fear get in the way. The impossible becomes the ordinary. I'm going to let go of you, but be careful, the ice is breaking. Do as I do. Follow me."

She shot across the ice, heading for the dam at the far end of the lake. The ice thinned to a paper-thick film as the distance between them widened. She leapt into the sky, turned a somersault in the air, and disappeared. He imagined himself as an Olympic skater and the blades on his feet grew in length. The shoreline passed by in a gray blur as the sound of breaking ice filled his ears. Raji flew over the spillway of the dam and tumbled down into the cascade. As panic mounted, he gathered his resolve and threw his arms before him, suddenly veering upward to the spot in the night sky where she had passed from sight.

The music of birdsong permeated the air where he hovered outside an open bedroom window as a globe of light. She sat up in her bed and yawned. "Raji, are you there?"

"Yes, outside the window. But I don't have a sheath yet."

"I'd feel better talking to someone with a body. You're a doctor. Or were a doctor. I suppose you've seen it all, haven't you? Don't be shy."

He floated in with the breeze that fluttered the curtains and imagined hands and feet, then filled in at the foot of the bed. "When we were skating together, what was that place, Annie?"

She tried to hold the memory of skating on the moon's reflection as other parts of the dreamscape faded. "It was Silver Lake when I was a girl," she said. My family had a house on the lake, and I would skate all day long—and into the evening— if it stayed cold enough."

She threw off the covers and sensors in the wall detected her motion. "Good morning, Annie, can I help you," said HOUBBS, the household built-in butler system.

"Lights on, please, HOUBBS. Make us some breakfast. I'll have my usual coffee and yogurt. How about you, Raji?"

"What would you like, sir?" asked the HOUBBS voice.

"Nothing complicated. The same."

"Black coffee and peach flavored yogurt. Please confirm."

Annie rolled her eyes. "Yes, the usual." On her way to the closet, she looked at herself in the mirror. Besides figure skating, she had been on the swimming team in high school and college and was still fit. While she was reaching into her closet, the doctor looked out the window. She pulled out a lightweight sweatshirt and jogging pants and put them on.

They made their way to the kitchen where breakfast waited on the counter. HOUBBS was the latest in smart house technology. Annie explained she was glad she had bought it because she was among the first in the country to have it installed and recommended it to her investor clients as a hot stock to buy. It made them a lot of money.

After jogging and eating breakfast, she picked out a conservatively cut Nippon suit with diagonal bands of bold colors, then slipped on a pair of Ballys and brushed her hair. "Would you like to see where I work, Raji?"

"I'm all in. Lead on."

"HOUBBS, lockdown," she said, directing him down the walk to her Alfa Spider. The sleep doctor watched her diamond ring scrape the anodized metal surface of the vehicle's skin as though through a magnifying glass, reminding him he was lucid. It left a mark next to the other dozen digs. Then the tires chirped. A smooth whine grew in pitch as she sped to work.

They reached the firm of Bancroft and Peckner and walked into an opulent foyer. The security guard smiled. "Good morning, Ms. Walker. Good morning, Dr. Batsunappan." Annie nodded and led her companion through the lobby and out into a wilderness of clustered desks peopled with traders, speculators, and hedgers.

The room, as long as a football field, was ringed with private offices for senior brokers along the outer walls. An air of anticipation hovered over it like a haze, as though the future was about to happen. The market wouldn't open for half an hour until the giant buzzer at the far end announced it. As she guided the doctor through the desks to her private office, the hungry energy continued building.

She sat down at her mahogany desk and pressed her thumb into the computer's security pad. "Please have a seat," she said, pointing to a plush chair. "I've got to go through these transaction requests before the market opens. Won't be too long."

She reviewed the requests feverishly to ensure they were done in time, then prepared for the meeting with her first client. "He's going to want some hot new tech stocks," she mumbled aloud. Slipping a translucent glove on each hand, she pulled up Walker's Manual Online and searched for Clear Light Sleep Technologies, a stock her research friend, Lynn Thomas, had recommended.

"Good choice," said Dr. Batsunappan.

COMPANY DESCRIPTION

Clear Light Sleep Technologies provides personal fulfillment through dream enhancement services and sleep therapy to people with sleeping disorders. Established 2029 with clinics in Baltimore and New York which provide comprehensive therapeutic facilities and expertise.

COMMENTS

The company executed a 0.260849 for 1 reverse split on January 9, 2031. All per share amounts have been adjusted for consistency. *INVESTMENT CLASSIFICATION*: Growth and Value.

As Annie moved Clear Light to the top of her best picks list, the buzzer declared the opening of the market. The desks were fully populated now, and every phone line was busy. John Glauss, a handsome dark-haired man the same age as Annie, sat outside her doorway drumming his fingers nervously on his desk. He held up a bottle of 1959 Lafite-Rothschild and shouted, "Care for a glass of wine over lunch?"

A pencil flew by his head and bounced off the wall. He shrugged and began typing as a paper plane crash-landed on his desk. She sighed and shook her head.

Annie turned to the doctor. "I have an appointment now. I know this is rude, but could you disappear until we're done. It's private."

The doctor looked at her wistfully. "You mean that literally, don't you." She nodded and he rose and walked out the door. Standing behind John Glauss, he smiled to her over his shoulder, then vanished into John's head.

"Raji?" Annie whispered. John winked.

Dr. Gottlieb strutted imperiously down the hallway and stooped to pick up the pencil which had landed near John's desk. "You guys are crazy. This is worse than Romper Room." He stepped into Annie's office and she shook his hand, then closed the door.

"You have to be out of your mind to work here," said Annie, "I'm fully qualified." He had brought in several new clients to Annie and she wanted to make him feel appreciated. "Can I get you anything? Coffee or Danish?"

"No thanks. What do you have for me?" He sat in the easy chair, which creaked beneath his weight.

"I found several winners for you. They have risk but could yield thirty percent or more. This one, Clear Light Sleep Technologies, could make a killing. I'm buying some for myself."

He leaned forward. "What's so good about it?"

"With all the stories about sleep deficit replacing cancer and heart disease as the nation's worst killers, Clear Light is positioned to experience explosive growth. There's a bill before Congress to fund more research for sleeping disorders. When that passes, the sky's the limit. It'll be a whole new bubble."

"Sounds like a possible contender," said Gottlieb. "But what if it doesn't pass? What else we got?"

Annie ran through her other picks, then he announced his decision. "Sleep care and neurological electronics. I'll do $5,096,000 for 5,200 shares of Clear Light Sleep Technologies, and

$5,000,000 for 3,300 shares of Neurologic Systems, the one with the liquid metal synthetic organs."

Her lips curled into a smile. "Excellent. Good picks."

"Hold on," he chortled. "Hedge 'em for short selling."

"You must know something I don't. Can you let me in on it? Doctor."

Gottlieb leaned back into the cushions with a tight smirk on his face. "Nope."

She nodded. "I respect your privacy, and I do appreciate your business. Let me take you out to lunch, anywhere you want to go."

"I've got to catch the maglev to Washington. Just keep your eyes open and keep me posted." He was out the door without saying goodbye.

Annie danced her way to the market floor, her endorphins raging off the scale. She held up her fingers in John Glauss's face. "$10 million, Raji," she said, wiggling them, then kissing him fully on the lips.

He looked at her in bewilderment. "Gadzooks!"

"What's wrong. Aren't you happy for me? I made a lot of money for a few minutes work. Let's open that bottle of grape juice."

"Of course I am, but you can't imagine how much you helped me. That coot is the source of my troubles, but you couldn't have known. Now I know why he's trying to destroy me."

"I don't understand what you mean." She looked up at the numbers flying by on the wall near the ceiling, then stared blankly at Raji. "The ticker just dropped 10,000 points."

"It's bad news, isn't it?" he asked. "Should you cancel the order?"

"No. Only he can do that. It's actually a positive. He hedged it. A little nudge will send Clear Light over the threshold, but I'm not worried. Tomorrow morning the market will be back up there." She touched her forehead. "Do you ever get a feeling of deja vu?"

"Not me. It's a form of precognition, but I see where you're coming from. I'm going to pull out of this dream and get myself a lawyer. There's business I need to take care of."

"Good luck, Raji. I hope I see you again." But she was speaking to John who had a startled look on his face. She laughed. "Everything okay?"

Annie wound her way through the maze of desks as alerts flashed on computer screens. She overheard a floor manager admonishing his team to unload. When she poked her head inside the door of Lynn's office, Lynn looked up from her screen and rubbed her neck. "Come on in. What have you been up to?"

"I just sold $10 million," Annie exclaimed. "Thanks for the tip on Clear Light."

"Don't mention it," said Lynn.

"Let me take you out to lunch. We need to celebrate."

"I'd love to, but I can't leave my desk. The place is going crazy"

Annie skipped lunch and entered her sale into the system. Her manager, Dave Morton, stopped in to congratulate her. Dave was a likeable person. He seldom gave an order, directing by humorous anecdotes instead. Those under him cringed in fear whenever he withheld his sense of humor.

"You're the number one producer for the third straight quarter. You made the Hundred Percent Club. Keep doing what you're doing," he said.

"Thanks Dave," she said, beaming.

"What do you think is going to happen with this panic?"

"Tomorrow the president will appoint a new FED chair who will cut the prime rate. Buy the fuck out of everything."

He nodded as a smile spread over his face. "I'll pass that around. See you at the Jefferson tonight. Brenton Technologies puts out quite a spread."

"See you there," said Annie.

She teleconferenced and juggled transactions all afternoon. Most clients thought a major market crash was imminent and wanted to change their portfolios, but Annie stuck to her premonition.

It's your chance to buy low and get a bargain, she told them. She was the maker of wealth, there to fulfill their material dreams and her own. Dave Morton spoke to the traders on the floor, telling them there would be a rate cut the next morning. John Glauss and Lynn Thomas followed Annie's lead. When the buzzer sounded the close of the market the coffers of Bancroft and Peckner were wide open and poised for a feeding frenzy the next day.

"Find a safe spot," she told the valet, handing him the keys to the Alpha. She walked into the Jefferson Hotel a little past seven. It had nearly burned to the ground in 1901, but the lofty glass ceiling in the lobby had survived intact despite the fire. The epicurean décor and faux marble columns lent an air of elegance and symmetry.

She saw Lynn standing by the statue of an alligator and waved. They exchanged greetings and proceeded down the ante-bellum stairways toward the lower dining halls. Annie wore a black oriental gown and a diamond necklace. Lynn wore an elegant green dress and a sapphire ring on each hand. Heads turned as they entered.

Dave Morton, his wife, and John Glauss were sitting at a table at the far end. John helped seat them. "You are stunning," he told Annie as he sat down beside her.

Dinner was excellent and the conversation pleasant. Afterward, a Brenton spokesman took to the podium near Annie's table as dessert was served. He delivered a clever speech regarding the company's place in the industry and the future ahead, then announced a new product. "Nothing like this has ever been done before and we're proud to have pioneered it," he told the guests. "It's called recombinant metal crystallography and it's based on the human DNA model. Think of it as an organic metal that can be programmed to take on whatever shape the coded instructions give it. In its pre-program state the organic metal is a fluid that can be injected into any part of an organism without triggering an immune response. When it reaches its destination, the program is activated and the organic metal crystals take on structure. RMC can be used in cardiology to rebuild heart chambers or arteries without rejection issues. In neurology, it can integrate with damaged nerves or repair lesions to restore electrical pathways. There are hundreds of applications."

The audience clapped enthusiastically. When Annie got home afterward, she threw her gown over a hook and kicked her shoes off. Moments later she was asleep in bed.

When she awoke, she realized she hadn't told HOUBBS when to wake her. The clock said 8:30. She grabbed the first comfortable thing in the closet and yanked it on as she fought through piles of shoes to find a matching pair. "HOUBBS: diet Bzzz and a sugarless donut."

She splashed water on her face, ran to the kitchen, downed the Bzzz in three swallows, grabbed the donut and stuffed it down on the way to the car. "HOUBBS: lockdown."

Annie punched the pedal and was down the road in two seconds. She set a record getting to work and ran through the lobby before the guard could notice.

The buzzer sounded as she passed a cart laden with donuts and beverages. She grabbed another donut and an Ultra Steam, the artificial aspartame taste giving her a feeling of exhilaration as she forced it down.

A news flash appeared on the bottom of her computer screen after logging in. The president announced a new Fed chair and confirmed her premonition of a rate cut. As a shout of joy formed on her lips she felt a huge pressure at the back of her head. She gasped, took two steps away from the desk, then fell to the floor, teetering drunkenly on all fours. It took several minutes to gather enough strength to get up and slump down in the easy chair. A fog filled her mind from the neuro toxins flooding through her blood brain barrier. There were two of everything and the room was heaving up and down.

John Glauss noticed her struggling and burst in. "What's the matter?"

"I have an awful headache. It starts to make sense. Do you believe in deja vu?" She tried to remember what Raji had taught her. She had to get back to the lake and held her hands before her. "I will awaken within the dream and know... and know... " But she had four hands. John's eyes darkened into sunken hallows, his face becoming emaciated and rotten. She summoned all her willpower and intent, but the figure towered above, leering at her and blocking the way out of the loop.

5

Dr. Batsunappan fluttered his eyelids to break the sleep crust that had formed and noticed the memory fob containing his latest updates to Portal 2.0 and the Journal of Neurology was gone from the night table. He heard the voices of Gottlieb and Mark Payne at the foot of the bed and hoped Mark had slipped it in his pocket.

"I just heard from Brenton Technologies that the code looks good," said Dr. Payne.

"What else would you expect them to say? Tell them to keep looking," said Gottlieb. "And transfer Ann Taylor to Bayview Critical Care. It's better equipped for long term. Him too."

"The ward's full. They'll be okay here on IVs." Mark turned the lights out and closed the door behind them.

Raji realized Gottlieb wasn't worried about anyone's health. Some of the patients in the neurosciences coma ward had been there for years. He and Annie would be as good as dead with the right mix of coma cocktails in their veins. But was Mark lying? There were always a few empty beds. Mark was his best ally and Raji didn't want to doubt his motives. Both the waking world and the dream world were illusory and either could be false. There were different paths to take to discover the truth but which? Trained as a scientist, he knew science was sometimes illusory and over time its truths changed and misled. He thought of the Mahayana path of emptiness that led to the ultimate nature of things, then hestitated for fear that he was in monkey-sleep.

In the dark, still resting on his palm, he turned within himself, calling to Lama Sri Dorbu. A long-haired robed figure appeared in the darkness. "I fear I have deluded myself. Help me find the path to truth, Guruji.

The yogi hovered with an sfumato smile. "The Buddha taught us 'all things are like a dream, like an illusion, like a bubble, like a shadow, like a dewdrop, like a lightening flash; you should contemplate them thus.' We create our own suffering and misery because we are unawakened. You have already found the right path. To help free others, show them the covering of ignorance and what lies beneath. That is the cause of their grief."

The figure dissolved and the sleep doctor found himself in a place without form or color, a gray abstract of nothingness. Concentrating on the backs of his lids, he formed himself as a sheathless globe and rose to the space between his eyes. A dream manufactured itself and he watched it unfold.

A trailer with faded lettering on the sides reading AASHTO sat on a parking lot of the southbound side of the Maryland House rest stop. Inside were ten stern faced people watching a man working at a control console on the wall. "We have a new tool in our arsenal, a magic crystal," the man said, making adjustments as he paused between each word. He turned to face his audience to make sure they were listening. It was Mark Payne.

"We've got a lot on the plate so let's get on with it," demanded a medal-bedecked general.

Standing by the general was Director Drendlen, a sallow-complexioned man with puffy lips and thick spectacles. "The committee has been briefed on the Maryland House Project already, doctor. What we need is a demonstration. If it works, we'll buy it. Very simple. Everyone here has clearance, so go ahead, speak freely."

Dr. Payne took a deep breath and slowly exhaled. "I'll be to the point. Kennen crystal satellites are obsolete. They're too expensive and ineffective beyond reading license plates or counting tanks on the ground. With Director Drendlen's permission, I'll demonstrate a radically new system that will totally change intelligence gathering. Our magic crystal is no longer a satellite orbiting overhead, second guessing what's going on. It's in the middle of the action, implanted inside a subject's head; looking, hearing, feeling everything he or she interacts with."

"Are you talking about some kind of bug?" asked a thin man in a dark suit.

"In a sense, yes, but it communicates neurological signals in both directions, not just audio-video." There was silence. "It goes far beyond conventional bugs. It's a high-performance, bi-directional brain-machine interface and manipulates thoughts, too. The best thing is to show you."

A map of the Washington – Baltimore corridor popped up on the screen showing a vehicle approaching the rest stop from the northbound lane of Route 95.

"Director Drendlen has identified a known subversive named George Anders to use for our demonstration. He's a keynote speaker at the workers protest march in Philadelphia. Anders is the president of the Worldwide Worker's Union Mid-Atlantic Division. We've ID'd his car on the GPS grid and surveillance records show that he often stops here when traveling Route 95. When he enters the travel center we'll implant the interface, monitor the subject's activity, then alter his speech and actions to produce whatever consequences are deemed appropriate by Director Drendlen."

The committee members pulled up their seats in a semi-circle in front of the console as the lights dimmed. Dr. Payne stepped to the side and pointed at the control console. "Ladies and gentlemen, I give you the Maryland House Project." They watched through surveillance cameras as George Anders disconnected from the GPS traffic stream and diverted into the parking lot with a dozen other cars. He squeezed into a spot about 400 meters from the northbound ramp. He and his wife, Alice, melded into the other travelers heading for the entrance doors. As they entered, they passed by an antique penny flattening machine.

"Who would want to flatten a penny?" asked George.

"I thought they stopped making them," Alice replied.

"Me too. Let's meet back here."

She veered toward the ladies' room and George made his way to the men's. He scanned the wall, frantically looking for an opening until he picked a urinal with only two in line. When his turn came, he stepped forward and let the dam break. A camera mounted in the ceiling zoomed in on the back of his head which transmitted to the high-resolution display in the trailer.

"This is the implant," said Dr. Payne, pointing to three fine hairs falling from the scalp onto George's collar.

"We're not catching it, Doctor," said Drendlen. "Can you point it out?"

The camera zoomed in closer. A nanobot insect, less than the size of a gnat, deposited a dot smaller than a pore on George's scalp. The dot burrowed into his head without a trace. "We borrowed a UAS—a nano drone—from DARPA N3 for the delivery. That part of the technology is already proven. But the little dot you all just saw is why you're here today. It's the latest in piezoelectric liquid crystallography. It liquefies, finds its way through the scalp and bone, and enters the brain. We activate the interface and everything going on inside the subject's head is

transmitted back to us." Dr. Payne pushed a button on the panel. "Anders is our eyes and ears."

George was busy with the business at hand. For a split second he felt something like a mosquito bite on the back of his head. He forgot about it at once, it passed so quickly. The perspective shifted from the ceiling to a point two feet from the wall and the sound of flushing was heard.

"Excuse me," said George, pulling up his fly and backing away from the urinal, side stepping the man behind him.

"So, what's supposed to happen?" asked the general. "I only see some guy taking a leak."

"That's the beauty of it, General," said Dr. Payne. "It's undetectable and the implant is so small there's no pain or mark. And we all shed a little sometimes." The bald general frowned but Dr. Payne plowed on. "It happened already. You aren't looking through the camera anymore, you're inside the subject's head, experiencing what he experiences, seeing what he sees. His brain waves are being sent to us right now, here in this room, and translated by our system into human terms of perception like sight, sound and feelings."

The audience remained silent. Dr. Payne was fearful he had lost them. "That's only a part of what it can do." He extended a metal pointer and tapped on an area of the console filled with graphs. "These depict emotional and psychological states. This is the strength of input and output signals from the subject's brain to our control center here. This one indicates serotonin levels, pain, pleasure, motivation, and last, but not least, sexual stimulation."

"What's the range of this thing?" asked the thin man.

"Unlimited. As long as Starnet is operational."

"You mentioned it manipulates thoughts and actions. How does that work?"

"Good question," said Dr. Payne. "Back in the 1980's a British researcher named Greene identified the parts of the human nervous system that send and receive nerve impulses. Greene was ahead of his time. He hooked up the outputs of his own nerves to those of paraplegics and was able to control their limbs. In another experiment he connected electrodes embedded in a patient's brain to a computer and trained him to move the cursor across the screen. Recently we developed the technical components to put his research to use in the brain interface but without the wires. We incorporated it into our own system using something called a neuro-translator, then monitor the subject's brain patterns, digitize them, rearrange them and play back our modified version to create the thoughts, speech, or actions that we choose. It's their own modified brain pattern, so they can't detect the change. They're under our control and never know it."

Helen Buffini, a legal counsel to the National Security Committee, rose indignantly from her seat. "Dr. Payne, really. Mind control?"

"Let's call it manipulation. It influences sex drive, mood, outlook, and sleep too."

"We could shoot this thing into the heads of the enemy from the air and march 'em right back the hell home," said the general.

Director Drendlen smiled. "Or control our own armies from this trailer. There are enormous possibilities. We've only just begun learning what it can do."

"Director Drendlen," said the counselor.

He leaned toward the general, continuing to ignore her. "General, while Mr. Anders is on his way to the demonstration..."

"Director Drendlen," she repeated angrily.

Drendlen scowled. "What, Ms. Buffini, what?"

"This is barbaric. Illegal. A violation of free speech."

"Thank you for sharing your opinion but, no, it's top secret medical research."

"How far do you imagine this can go until there's a scandal? I have to inform you as legal counselor you are on thin ice."

"No chance. It's classified and won't ever leave this room. It's medical research, funded with blessings from the highest places."

The committee continued to watch the display. George and Alice returned to their car and drove to the exit ramp where they went on autopilot and synced to the grid.

"You want to go over your speech again? I'll read along," said Alice.

"You always get sick reading in the car."

She pulled up the document on her phone. "No, I don't. Go ahead."

George's face grew serious, then he looked up as he remembered the words he had prepared:

"I'm honored to be here today. Honored that you, my fellow workers, have asked me to speak on your behalf on this cold day, about something we all share; the right to a livelihood, to a decent standard of living; to fair labor laws that ensure uniform standards of decency for all people throughout the world.

"We are the Worldwide Workers Union. Everywhere on this globe, in every continent, we have fought for the rights of all workers to be safe and healthy and to receive decent wages, training, and education to maintain the highest professional standards. We stand for the end of child labor and the abolishment of prison labor.

"More importantly, we stand united and determined that this administration will not succeed in its attempts to abolish labor unions and take us back to the past which we had fought so hard to escape from. We must move forward. We must not rest until the unregulated toil of children and the under trodden is eliminated from the face of the earth. It's our duty to elevate the social conscience of leadership for the betterment of all members of society…"

"You getting this, Payne?" asked Drendlen.

"It's recording into memory right now," the doctor replied.

Director Drendlen faced the committee. "We're all on the same page here. This is not the message we want broadcast around the globe. It must be stopped in its tracks and it will, now that we have the tool. The Maryland House Project will succeed. It's vital to our national interest. Thank you for your time. We'll reconvene tomorrow."

"I think Buffini doesn't like the project," Dr. Payne commented sadly after she had left.

"She's got to play ball or she's out of a job. Do we have the whole speech, Doctor?"

"He's finished. We can start the modification."

"Play it back, then start feeding him some behavioral reinforcements that will make him more like—one of us."

"Behavior modification is a gradual thing. But we can have him reciting our corrected version of his speech right now."

The director listened intently and wrote on a notepad as the speech played back.

"He's in Philadelphia now," said Dr. Payne. "It's a half hour until start time."

Drendlen handed the altered version to Dr. Payne. "Here. Plug in these changes."

Minutes later someone stepped out of a bagel shop and directed the activists into a tight parking spot on Front Street.

"Look who that is, it's Larry Phillips," sneered Drendlen. "Damned terrorist. You saving all this?"

"Everything."

"We were turned down for a permit again," said Larry, holding the door for George as he struggled to pull his bulk from the car.

"Fuck 'em. You can't arrest 450,000 protestors."

"They'll reach Penn's Landing in a few minutes."

"We better get to the stage then," said George.

They walked down Front Street to the aluminum scaffolding of the stage as the marchers came into view. The police had erected fences along the sidewalks and intersections, packing the demonstrators more densely in the street. The crowd stretched back from the landing as far as the eye could see. Display screens hung from poles at the intersections. Mainstream media and podcast cameras swept in to capture the event.

Larry and George moved to the podium as the marchers filled up the landing and came to a halt. The air swelled with protest chants as snow began falling through the frigid air. Phillips raised his hands and leaned into the mics. "My friends. Thank you for coming to show your support for our cause. You endured a long march through the wind and cold today. Each one of you began your journey with a single step. You marched here one step at a time. That's how we'll win back our rights; one heart and one mind at a time. Brothers and sisters, we shall not stop until there is fairness and equality for all! Thank you for your perseverance and for your commitment." He waited for the cheers to die down.

"Here to kick off this event is our president of the WWU Mid-Atlantic Region, USA, George Anders!"

George lumbered to the podium and looked down at the long blocks of humanity standing silently in the falling snow. Alice's upturned face looked into his from below the foot of the stage. They exchanged smiles through the snowflakes. He faced the crowd and opened his mouth to speak.

Drendlen stabbed at the display with his finger. "Now."

Dr. Payne nodded. "Transmitting."

"I am honored to be here today," said George. "You, my fellow workers, have asked me to speak on your behalf about something we all share; the right to a decent standard of living and to laws that ensure uniform standards of decency for all people. But I've been thinking long and deeply on the Worldwide Workers Union and its goals and course of action. After much consideration, I've re-evaluated my position. I have come to believe we are on the wrong road to achieve the things we need."

A contentious murmur arose.

George wore his usual cherubic look, seemingly unconcerned. Larry cupped his hand and spoke into his ear. "I hope the punch line is good."

George continued, looking believable and convincing. "We carry within us the seeds of creativity. We have the right to exercise it, the right to innovate, the right to build and to succeed. The spark that has made this land great is within each of us; we are all Titans, every one of us. Do we want to regulate the spark and put out the flame? Are we all really the same or do we each have a free will? What're you afraid of? I'll tell you what you're afraid of...."

A shoe struck George on the chest. He picked it up and turned it over slowly, bewilderment spreading across his face. "We're afraid of hoping for more." He dropped the shoe and looked at the crowd. "We need to trust in leadership that has the vision and courage to deliver back to us what has been stolen, the rights of the individual."

"Traitor," a protester cried. "That's fucking crap." "How much they payin' you, brother?" yelled another.

Larry grabbed George by the shoulder and forced him back from the mics. "Thank you, George, that's enough of that."

"I'm not finished," said George, struggling back to the mics. Larry and an aide shoved him away.

"You're finished," Larry snarled. "Get him out of here."

The aide grabbed George's arm and forced him down the stairs. Larry shot down behind him a moment later. "After all the years I've known you, why now, at this moment? You never said a word to me or anyone else about crossing the floor."

George's eyes opened wide. "What the hell are you talking about?"

"That wasn't the speech you were going to give," said Alice. She unfolded her copy of the script and repeated his lines. "George, don't you know what you just said?"

"I never said that."

The crowd milled forward and forced aside a barrier, surrounding George and Alice. "You're working for them now. Who's payin' you, traitor?"

"What? Nobody," said George.

A burly steelworker pushed him and cocked his fist. Alice screamed and started running as the others held him back. The police barreled through, pushing people aside with their storm shields. Alice and George ran down the street and disappeared into the snow while the police battled an insurrection of angry marchers.

Director Drendlen and Dr. Payne sat at a table in the travel center eating dinner as the seven o'clock news aired on a TV nearby. Standing in front of a burning police car, the commentator began her report:

"A demonstration by the Worldwide Workers Union has ended in mayhem as hundreds of demonstrators wrestle with police. Trash cans have been emptied to create bonfires in the middle of intersections and the police car in back of me, one of dozens, was set on fire. Tear gas was used to subdue the unruly agitators. Dozens of arrests have been made. The violence began shortly after the keynote speaker, George Anders, denounced the direction the WWU has been taking and advocated a return to individual, not collective rights. An agitator had to be pulled away from manhandling Mr. Anders, who fled with a woman, presumably his wife. His whereabouts is unknown. Sandy King reporting live from Penn's Landing, Philadelphia."

Dr. Payne smiled. "The doctor knows best. Care to place an order?"

"That went well but can you change his behavior?"

"It's like training a dog," replied the doctor. "Reward him for good behavior. Only instead of a pat on the head, we feed him pleasure directly into his brain. We learn his pleasure frequencies then redirect them back. It can be better than an orgasm or heroin rush. We regulate the level of pleasure depending on the kind of reinforcement we need. He'll want to act in the way that brings the greatest pleasure or prevents it from ending."

The director became cordial. "Tell me, how far can we take this thing? I mean, it could be used in a lot of ways, right?"

Dr. Payne cracked open a mussel shell. "It has great potential in medicine and psychotherapy. I'm working on an app that runs the console on your cell phone. There's almost no limit."

"What is it that you want out of all of this?"

A series of squishy sounds ensued, followed by a thick swallow. "Just recognition."

"Recognition like going down in medical history, you mean?"

"Everything else will follow. Funding. My own company."

The director drummed his fingers on the table and leaned closer. "Now me, I just want to serve my country. By protecting it. The project is bigger than you and me but it's a double-edged sword—like when we learned to split the atom. Some good came out of it, but it got in the wrong hands." He placed his hand on the doctor's shoulder. "We have to make sure it stays in the right hands. It's in the national interest. It stays in the committee and goes nowhere else. I want your word on that."

The doctor frowned and scooped the flesh from another mussel.

"I'll see you get the recognition you deserve. When Buffini gets here tomorrow, I want you to give her a little bug bite."

Dr. Payne nodded reluctantly.

Helen Buffini had arranged for Sandy King and her news crew to meet outside the AASHTO trailer at nine in the morning. George, Alice, and Larry joined them.

The reporter nodded to the cameraman. "Mr. Anders, I'm glad you agreed to meet with us. Let me explain to our viewers that Mr. Anders, many of you may remember him from the demonstration in Philadelphia yesterday, has claimed he is the victim of a government mind control experiment conducted upon him from this trailer in the parking lot here at the Maryland House travel center near Exit 80 in Aberdeen."

The camera focused on George. "I have trouble believing it myself, but the speech was not my speech. The public must understand that. Ms. Buffini informed me I'm a victim of mind control by our government."

The camera panned back to the reporter. "Ms. Helen Buffini is a legal advisor to the National Security Council and has taken on the role of whistle blower. She agreed to talk with us about these allegations." She held the mic toward the counselor.

"It's true," Helen Buffini confirmed. "There are issues here which need to be brought to the public's attention. They're testing a neuro-translator brain interface on Mr. Anders without his knowledge or consent. This experiment is an invasion of Mr. Anders's personal privacy and a violation of freedom of speech. They call it the Maryland House Project and they're testing to see of it could be extended to members of the military or political opponents of the administration."

"Is it true that this is classified top secret? Aren't you breaking the law by breaking the code of silence regarding classified government projects?"

"I'm willing to do the right thing, no matter what the cost," the counselor replied. She led the group to the trailer door and punched in the code for the lock. She heard a high-pitched buzzing as the door opened and in that instant realized it was too late. Dr. Payne and the director greeted them.

Drendlen instructed Dr. Payne to turn off the display screens and forced a smile. "Ms. Buffini, what are you doing bringing these people in here? You know this is a classified project."

Sandy King stuck the mic in his face. "Director Drendlen, Mr. Anders claims he's the victim of a medical experiment to control his thoughts and speech. Is this true? Would you care to comment?" She scratched at the back of her head, wondering why mosquitos were out in the wintertime.

"I'm not commenting on anything. You've entered a classified area without clearance. Leave here at once." He slammed the door shut.

A quadcopter landed and let off men in ghillie suits onto the asphalt. An unmarked van pulled up and they whisked the newsmakers inside.

"Are we going to be on the news tonight?" asked Larry, buckling his seat belt dutifully.

The cameraman shook his head. "No. We can't use the video. It's scrambled and the sound was wiped somehow."

"Nothing to show," said Sandy King in a deadpan.

"No proof without audio," replied the counselor.

But none of that seemed to matter.

Inside the trailer, Drendlen hung his arm on the doctor's shoulder. "Thank you, Mark. I knew I could count on you."

6

The atmosphere heated as the figures in the van faded to translucency. They hung in the air briefly before extinguishing as the oneironaut hovered in the nothingness of the place of emptiness. A voiceless vibration called his name. Intuition told him it was Annie. The moment he remembered her he passed through the moon and floated down its chute of light into his body on the ice of Silver Lake. "Annie," he answered. Sweeping the dreamscape, he spotted something small scurrying through the brush on the shore.

By the time he reached the opening in the bushes where he saw it, it was gone. Billowing clouds shapeshifted into a black anvil above the trees and forged into his consciousness the image of the house in Annie's first nightmare. He willed himself through the woods and found the iron gates. The house was at the end of the long driveway, exactly as it appeared before. It boomed with empty echoes as he struck the thick door with the knocker. "Raji?" said a tiny voice.

"Yes. Can I come in?"

She slammed the door shut when he stepped inside and clasped him tightly. "You were gone so long I thought you weren't coming back."

Her glowing energy had gone and she appeared wan and weak. The doctor rocked her soothingly. "I wouldn't desert you." She was trembling despite the oppressive heat in the house. "Tell me what's the matter."

"I've lost control. I can't leave here, but at least I'm safe."

"From what? What are you afraid of?"

Annie sank to the floor and contorted into a tortured ball of tangled limbs at his feet. "I don't know." At first no sound came out, then she heaved a deafening lung gush of despair into the air, shaking him to his core.

He let her cry for several long moments, then looked down at her compassionately, wondering what could have led to such a level of distress. Her personal inner turbulence was too great to jump her sheath. "What does this house mean to you?" he asked.

"I grew up here."

"Come," he said, gently pulling her up and guiding her to a mirror hung on the wall in the living room. "Show me yourself when you were a girl. Reach into the mirror and pull her out and show her to me."

She sobbed convulsively. "No. I can't."

"Sometimes we must confront what we fear most. Show me. Thrust your arm into the glass and pull her out."

Her fingertips rested briefly on her reflection, then the glass rippled and her hand penetrated into the glass. She groped inside until she felt a hand take hers, then distilled back into the room as a teenager dressed in a swimsuit.

"How old are you?" he asked.

"Thirteen."

"It looks like you're going swimming. Are your parents here?"

A wind gust rattled the windows and the sky darkened. Thunder growled in the distance. She shook her head. "They're at work."

He heard the sound of feet on the stairs. "Who's coming down the stairs?"

"Jimmy, my brother."

A small boy bolted past them and out the door. "Wait, Jimmy, it's going to rain," she yelled and ran after him with the doctor at her heels. Jimmy raced down the garden path to a swimming pool and canon-balled into the deep end, laughing. When Annie reached the patio, the heavy skies spilled open in a downpour. They heard a tearing sound and deafening boom as lightning struck the iron gates outside the fenced-in garden. Jimmy popped to the surface floating face down in the water.

A second flash enveloped them. When it had receded, Annie was sitting on the living room floor in front of the mirror shaking with anguish. The doctor squatted by her. Placing his palms on her temples, he rubbed them gently. "That was not easy. Thank you."

"It's my fault."

"Your only fault is that you loved him too much. Love can be an uplifter or a destroyer. Sometimes it deceives you into believing things that aren't true, but you could no more control what happened than you can stop the sun or the moon. Now that you've remembered, you must let go of that moment. Release the past and be free. Awaken from your dream. Return to the world of brick and mortar where your loved ones are waiting for you. There's no reason to dwell here anymore."

The EEG at Annie's monitoring station changed from double helix to sawtooth and then to beta waves. The technician sent an alert to Dr. Payne, but Dr. Batsunappan was already at her bedside.

Annie propped herself up. "Am I awake?"

Dr. Batsunappan beamed ecstatically. "Yes. Welcome back."

She stared blankly. "How long was I asleep?"

"Three days." He held out a notepad and pen and set them on the table. "Write down what you can remember from your last dream. Lie back down and think about the last few emotions you were feeling. Let the rest fill in. The house where you lived as a girl—the swimming pool. Your brother."

She sank back into her pillow for a moment then shook her head. "I never had a brother."

"I have to be honest with you." He looked her in the eye. "We were worried at first that it was the implant that was preventing you from waking up. You were in constant REM all that time, except for a new pattern we hadn't seen before. Now I believe the problem was created from something in your past, not the implant—a trauma you try to avoid remembering. Understanding the dream could help."

"It's just a blank."

"Go back further. To the stock exchange. Does the name Gottlieb sound familiar?"

Her eyes lit brightly. "Sure. He's my best client. He's a short seller."

He paced back and forth excitedly. "You mean, he's done business with you?"

"Yes. He bought tons of Clear Light stocks. That's how I knew about you."

A nurse walked into the room followed by Dr. Payne. "Look who's awake. Your EEG is back to normal, sweety, and your vitals are good." She turned to Dr. Batsunappan. "Should I disconnect her?"

He exhaled slowly then gestured impatiently to Dr. Payne. "You have to ask *him*."

"Based on what I just heard, yes. And get her discharge started." The surgeon smiled at Annie. "I'm sure she's ready to go home."

"Wait a minute, Mark." Dr. Batsunappan pulled him out into the hallway so they wouldn't be heard. "The device didn't malfunction; she's suffering from dissociative amnesia. She's suppressing a memory of a horrific event in her childhood and needs a psychiatrist. At least schedule a psychological evaluation before she leaves. It could reoccur."

Dr. Payne nodded. "Okay. But Gottlieb has to know. I don't want him to think I'm trying to sneak her out of here without telling him. You know how that old asshole thinks. Why don't we both pay him a visit right now?"

"Thanks, Mark." He patted him on the shoulder. "I knew I could count on you. One other thing. Do you know a legal counselor named Helen Buffini who works for the government?"

"I don't." His eyebrows knitted together. "Why?"

The sleep doctor's face softened. "You've taken a load off my mind. The world isn't ready yet for Portal 2.0. The technology could be dangerous in the wrong hands."

Dr. Payne regarded him quizzically. "That's your call, whatever the reason. I kept it in a safe place."

Gottlieb's office was severe in its appointments; just several dented filing cabinets and a splintered oak desk with two worn Queen Anne chairs set before it. The two physicians shifted uncomfortably on the lumpy padding of the seats. They fidgeted silently until he entered carrying a ream of papers which he plunked down unceremoniously. His knees popped as he lowered himself into his chair.

"To what do we owe this pleasure?" he asked.

Dr. Payne leaned forward. "An update on Ann Taylor. She's awake. Dr. Batsunappan believes her problem stems from a childhood trauma. She needs a psychological evaluation before she's released."

"Brenton Technologies must be informed there's nothing wrong with the program. The device worked perfectly," Dr. Batsunappan added.

Gottlieb glared with suspicion. "Why are you still here?"

A vein popped out on Dr. Batsunappan's forehead. He gripped the arms of his chair tightly. "The real question is, why are *you* still here? You've tried to prevent her from regaining consciousness. You've tried to sink any progress with Ann Taylor the whole time and I know why. I know all about your insider trading and short selling. You'll lose your millions if it gets out. We'll see who really gets his license suspended."

The old white hair massaged a tick on his cheek and let out a malodorous laugh. The papers on his desk began floating upward into the air. "Who will believe a quack like you? You are the one guilty of the insider trading. You are the one who already knew Ann Taylor. Don't you remember?"

"What is this, some kind of KGB projection technique? Are you part of this, Mark?" He watched the papers form a cloud on the ceiling.

"This is turning very bad, Raji," said Dr. Payne. "You should pull out now." He grasped Raji's arm and smiled compassionately. "Think back six months ago. Try to remember."

Gottlieb smiled. "The shortness of breath. You had complained of shortness of breath and you signed up for a stress test."

His eyes darted frantically from one physician to the other. "No. I remember none of this." He pulled a floating page from the air and read the hand lettering written diagonally across it in magic marker: CARDIAC ARREST/FIBROMAS OBSTRUCTING BLOOD FLOW.

Dr. Payne applied more pressure to his arm. "The widow maker. Recall the chest pain that radiated to your arms, your neck and down your back before you collapsed. Life support couldn't be started before you had gone five minutes without oxygen."

He felt himself grow heavy when the grip on his arm released and forced himself to his feet as a high-pitched siren signaled flatline, but he couldn't hear its drone. Three women greeted him in the waiting room as he tried to escape. He felt the radiance of their caring and compassion pouring out to him. Unsure if they were nurses or angels, he allowed them to guide him to the doorway and lead him gently into the corridor.

He walked slowly with a heaviness in his chest that was hard to carry. It was crowded and everyone in the unidirectional stream was passing him. He had always been proud of his quick stride but now he couldn't keep up. There were hundreds stretching into thousands ahead in the stream. Pausing to get his bearings, he noticed a Tibetan wind horse flag on the wall and felt a refreshing breeze. Encouraged, he rejoined the sentient flow and resumed his journey.

Suddenly he felt something being placed in his trouser pocket and reached his hand inside. It was his Portal 2.0 memory stick. As he turned it over inside the pocket, a feeling of relief came upon him, then he felt someone else's hand touch his. From the hand flowed warmth and energy. It passed into him and his body grew lighter. He intertwined his fingers and grasped firmly. Suddenly he was floating inside his pocket looking at the hand with magnified vision, as though through a microscope, feeling the warmth and sentience in the fingertips, nerve to nerve, floating inside the creases in its knuckles and the whorls on its palms. Something was flowing between their hands. He thought it might be love. But whose?

When he looked to his side someone was walking along with him. "Annie, is that you?"

Annie turned into the corpse of the phantasm and he reeled with horror. His terror extinguished the moment she turned back into herself, radiant and strong. "Are you okay?" he asked.

She began speaking very fast, but no words came from her lips. He realized she had a message, but it was beyond what any words could convey. It was joy. It was illumination beyond language. As a tear rolled down his cheek he let go of her hand and she was gone.

He walked along quietly with the others, feeling the breeze quicken. The passage grew brighter. His body was not heavy. The air became frigid and penetrated inside him, but he didn't feel cold. It blew through his cells, through his being, cleansing him. A doorway ahead radiated light. He let go and melted into the wind.

About

Place has always been central to J. Thomas Brown's writing, whether exploring worlds that have vanished or imagining those to come. His early life was shaped by constant moving. His father's wanderlust carried the family up and down the American East Coast and across the ocean to Sweden and England. They lived in several remarkable homes: a miller's house at an old gristmill, a converted barn, an Olympic gold medalist's residence on the Isle of Lidingo in the Stockholm archipelago, an English manor in Kent, and a Pennsylvania fieldstone house once used by George Washington as an infirmary.

Settling in Richmond, Virginia, Brown tempered his own wanderlust and focused on writing. During this period he became an oneironaut and practiced lucid dreaming. Using dreams recorded from the journal he kept, he wrote several short stories and later adapted and unified them into the novella Cutting Through. The title is taken from the Buddha's Diamond Sutra which refers to the use of transcendental wisdom as a sharp and indestructible sword to sever illusions, falsehoods, and attachments that obscure the true nature of reality.

He has co-produced local access television programs, coordinated poetry readings at the Richmond Public Library, and served as an editor and webmaster for the Virginia Writers Project. Brown continues to craft stories rooted in place and dreamscapes, drawing on a lifetime of observation to create narratives that bridge past, present, and future.

Publication

Brown's work spans poetry, fiction, memoir, and essays. His poems and short stories have appeared in numerous magazines, journals, and anthologies. Other works include Saint Elmo's Light: Collected Stories, Driving With Poppi: A Patremoir, Mooncalf and A Seed Too Deep poetry collections, and the novels The Rose of Heaven, Land Beneath the Lake, and The Hole in the Bone.

To connect with the author, visit www.jthomasbrown.com